## Learning to Read, Step by Step!

### Ready to Read  Preschool–Kindergarten
• big type and easy words • rhyme and rhythm • picture clues
For children who know the alphabet and are eager to begin reading.

### Reading with Help  Preschool–Grade 1
• basic vocabulary • short sentences • simple stories
For children who recognize familiar words and sound out new words with help.

### Reading on Your Own  Grades 1–3
• engaging characters • easy-to-follow plots • popular topics
For children who are ready to read on their own.

### Reading Paragraphs  Grades 2–3
• challenging vocabulary • short paragraphs • exciting stories
For newly independent readers who read simple sentences with confidence.

### Ready for Chapters  Grades 2–4
• chapters • longer paragraphs • full-color art
For children who want to take the plunge into chapter books but still like colorful pictures.

**STEP INTO READING®** is designed to give every child a successful reading experience. The grade levels are only guides; children will progress through the steps at their own speed, developing confidence in their reading. The F&P Text Level on the back cover serves as another tool to help you choose the right book for your child.

Remember, a lifetime love of reading starts with a single step!

*For Aunt Christine—D.M.*

*To my children, Sidesel Emilie, Gabriel,
and Rumle Michael—M.E.*

Visit us on the Web!
StepIntoReading.com
rhcbooks.com

Educators and librarians, for a variety of teaching tools, visit us at RHTeachersLibrarians.com

*Library of Congress Cataloging-in-Publication Data*
Names: Murray, Diana, author. | Engell, Mette, illustrator.
Title: Double the dinosaurs / by Diana Murray ; illustrated by Mette Engell.
Description: New York : Random House, [2020] | Series: Step into reading. Step 1 |
Audience: Ages 4–6. | Audience: Grades K–1. | Summary: In this story that introduces the fundamentals of addition and the concept of doubling, a swamp becomes quite crowded as the number of dinosaurs doubles each time, from one to sixty-four.
Identifiers: LCCN 2019041351 | ISBN 978-0-525-64870-3 (trade paperback) |
ISBN 978-0-525-64871-0 (library binding) | ISBN 978-0-525-64872-7 (ebook)
Subjects: CYAC: Stories in rhyme. | Addition—Fiction. | Multiplication—Fiction. |
Dinosaurs—Fiction.
Classification: LCC PZ8.3.M9362 Dp 2020 | DDC [E]—dc23

Printed in the United States of America
10 9 8 7 6 5 4 3 2 1

This book has been officially leveled by using the F&P Text Level Gradient™ Leveling System.

# Double the Dinosaurs

by Diana Murray

illustrated by Mette Engell

Random House 🏠 New York

Hot, sunny day.
Cool, muddy shore.
All is quiet.
Then suddenly . . .

# ROAR!

One jumbo dinosaur

heads for the swamp.

Double the dinosaur. . . .

# Double the STOMP!

Two romping dinosaurs
leap through the mud.

Double the dinosaurs. . . .

# Double the THUD!

Four roaring dinosaurs
skip, hop, and tumble.

Double the dinosaurs. . . .

Double the RUMBLE!

Eight playful dinosaurs,
quick as a flash!

Double the dinosaurs. . . .

# Double the SPLASH!

Sixteen loud dinosaurs
munch on some lunch.

# Double the dinosaurs. . . .

# Double the CRUNCH!

Thirty-two dinosaurs
yawning and roaring.

# Double the dinosaurs. . . .

# Double the SNORING!

Sixty-four dinosaurs,
cozy as any.

ZZZ

Double the dinosaurs. . . .

Stop! Way too many!
The swamp is too
crowded.
This is no fun!

Away they
all run . . .

. . . and then
there are none.